ZANE
and
FRIENDS

A Book About Diversity, Love, Respect and Kindness

DEBORAH ODOM SUTTON

To order additional copies of this book, contact:
Xlibris
844-714-8691
www.Xlibris.com
Orders@Xlibris.com

ISBN: Softcover   978-1-6698-5707-5
         EBook   978-1-6698-5706-8

Print information available on the last page

Rev. date: 04/22/2023

This book is dedicated to my grandson,
and kids all over the world.

Ages 2-8 years old.

My name is Zane.

I am happy to be ME.

These are my friends. They are special too!
God made each of us unique and
different, can't you see?
It does not matter the color of our skin.
We have lots of fun when we come to
share, learn and play together.

We have a special song we sing when we come together. We would like to share it with you. Will you sing it with us too!

(Clap your hands when singing this song to your own beat and tune)

We are special,
We are unique.

Yes we are,
Yes we are.

Come on and clap your hands to the beat.
We are different,
We are alike.

We are all special in God's eyesight.
We are all special in God's eyesight.

Hooray! Hooray! Hooray!

Our parents tell us that it is okay to be different and to be proud of who we are.

We should always love ourselves no matter how different we are.

My friends and I have a special poem we would like to share with you. Will you say it with us?

1 2 3
Look at me.
I am proud to be me.
We are all special can't you see.
Can we all live in harmony?

It does not matter the color of your skin; everyone should be treated with kindness and respect.

The world is a beautiful rainbow of many different colors of people and cultures. Let's embrace diversity and celebrate each other's differences.

My friends and I hope you enjoyed this book about love, respect, kindness and diversity. We can all do our part to help make the world a better place for every human being.

The Future Is In Our Hands.

Special words to remember.

This book belongs to Someone very special.

_____

Name

Printed in the United States
by Baker & Taylor Publisher Services